Gum Gang Cracks the Case

By Kyla Steinkraus

Illustrated by David Ouro

Rourke
Educational Media
rourkeeducationalmedia.com

www.rourkeeducationalmedia.com

Edited by: Keli Sipperley
Cover and Interior layout by: Jen Thomas
Cover and Interior Illustrations by: David Ouro

Library of Congress PCN Data

Gumshoe Gang Cracks the Case / Kyla Steinkraus
(Rourke's Mystery Chapter Books)
ISBN (hard cover)(alk. paper) 978-1-63430-381-1
ISBN (soft cover) 978-1-63430-481-8
ISBN (e-Book) 978-1-63430-576-1
Library of Congress Control Number: 2015933737

Printed in the United States of America, North Mankato, Minnesota

Dear Parents and Teachers:

With twists and turns and red herrings, readers will enjoy the challenge of Rourke's Mystery Chapter Books. This series set at Watson Elementary School builds a cast of characters that readers quickly feel connected to. Embedded in each mystery are experiences that readers encounter at home or school. Topics of friendship, family, and growing up are featured within each book.

Mysteries open many doors for young readers and turn them into lifelong readers because they can't wait to find out what happens next. Readers build comprehension strategies by searching out clues through close reading in order to solve the mystery.

This genre spreads across many areas of study including history, science, and math. Exploring these topics through mysteries is a great way to engage readers in another area of interest. Reading mysteries relies on looking for patterns and decoding clues that help in learning math skills.

Whether readers are reading the books independently or you are reading with them, engaging with them after they have read the book is still important. We've included several activities at the end of each book to make this both fun and educational.

Do you think you and your reader have what it takes to be a detective? Can you solve the mystery? Will you accept the challenge?

Rourke Educational Media

Table of Contents

Alex, Future World-Famous Scientist

On the first Wednesday morning of November, I crammed my science project and my trifold poster presentation in the back of Mom's minivan. I always liked Wednesdays because our third-grade class had science lab in the afternoon. But this Wednesday was probably the best ever in the history of Wednesdays at Watson Elementary. Not only did we have science lab, but that night at 6 p.m. was the school-wide Science Fair.

My name is Alex Price. My favorite subject in the whole world is science. I am pretty sure I will be a famous scientist when I grow up. To make sure I get enough training in, I practice doing experiments whenever I can. This is not Mom's favorite thing, especially when she finds neon-green goo in my hamper or moldy petri dishes under my bed. She is a good sport, but there are a lot of groans and headaches going on in my house.

Even though science lab is supposed to be after lunch, on Science Fair day we brought our projects into the lab first thing in the morning for safekeeping. Mom helped me carry my stuff in.

Our teacher, Miss Flores, directed us as we came in. "Good morning, Alex and Mrs. Price," she said to us. "Please put your project against the far wall in the right hand corner. It looks wonderful!" Miss Flores was my favorite teacher. Her name meant flower in Spanish, and I even thought she was pretty as a flower, too.

Mom lugged my project over to the table. She hugged me and kissed my forehead. Normally this would be horribly embarrassing, but she knew she could get away with it since today was such a special day. In addition to the Science Fair, Dad was coming home today after being on deployment with the navy for nine months. Mom was picking him up and bringing him straight to the school for tonight's program.

I wiggled out of Mom's bear hug. I shook her hand goodbye like a gentleman. "See you tonight, ma'am."

My friends Tully and Caleb set up their projects next to me. Tully stared at her project with her hands on her hips. She'd built a volcano. It was huge and painted pink and purple. She set a jar of baking soda and a bottle of vinegar next to her trifold poster. "Blue lava is supposed to come out, but I can't test it until it's being judged tonight. What if it doesn't work?"

"Don't worry, it'll work great," I said.

"I hope so," Tully said with a sigh. Tully was very fashionable, always wearing bright colors and pretty sparkly stuff. She was really smart, too. Her favorite subjects to be smart in were reading, writing, and organizing stuff.

"Okay guys," Caleb said. "What did the volcano say to his wife?"

Tully shrugged. "I give up."

"I lava you so much!" Get it?" Caleb cracked up laughing. Caleb loved to be funny. He was also ridiculously messy.

Tully put a ruler between her project and Caleb's. "Keep your mess on your side."

Caleb shrugged. "You can dish it out, but you can't take it with you."

"Do you even know what that means?" I asked.

"Sure I do. Hey, what do you think of my project?" Caleb's favorite thing was cars, so he'd done an experiment testing how various ramp heights affected the distance a Hot Wheel car traveled. He'd glued a car to a small ramp as a model and made a bunch of charts for his poster.

"Come see mine, Alex," my friend Ronald "Rocket" Gonzaga said. Rocket was the fastest kid in the whole third grade. His experiment tested different types of paper airplanes and how their wing design affected the distance they could fly.

"That is really cool," I told him.

"Thanks. I wanted to test my MegaAstroids, but my mom said crumpled-up paper balls didn't count as a science experiment. These are not really paper airplanes, but super-galactic spaceships."

"Over here, guys!" Lyra Ladsen called to us from across the room. Lyra was a fantastic singer and had no problem being really loud, so it was not a surprise that her project tested sound waves using water levels in glass cups.

Rocket, Caleb, Tully, Lyra and I were all best friends. But we were even better than best friends, because we were also all detectives. We'd been solving mysteries around school since second grade. The school secretary, Mr. Sleuth, even called us the Gumshoe Gang. A gumshoe is another name for a detective, so it fits us pretty well.

"Hey, whose is that over there?" Rocket asked. A group of kids were crowded around a project in the corner. We headed over to check it out.

Carys Johnson stood in front of her project. She'd built some kind of small robot out of a red plastic cup. There was a motor attached on the top of the cup. There were three markers taped with masking tape to the cup, with their pointy ends on a large piece of white paper. She'd glued on a set of big googly eyes and drew a toothy smile on the front of the cup.

"This is my robot, Picasso," Carys said. She flipped a switch on his motor, and Picasso began to spin around, leaving beautiful marker swirls on the paper wherever he went.

"Wow!" Tully said.

"That's great, Carys," I said. She was one of the best artists in the class, so it made total sense that she would build a robot that could draw.

"I bet you're going to win with that," Xavier said.

"If I were a judge, I'd vote for Picasso," Javier said.

Carys beamed. "That would be awesome. My dad said he'd double the prize money if I win. So I'd get the $50 for the prize, and $50 from Dad."

"Wow," Xavier said glumly. He frowned. "My dad said if I didn't get at least an A on this project, I'd be grounded from all electronics for a month. He didn't offer me any money at all if I won."

Tully turned to me. "I wouldn't count Alex out yet to win. Where's your project?"

Everybody looked at me. "I'll show you." I led them back over to my table. Mom said no to my first two choices. I wanted to test which household products are the most flammable. Then I wanted to compare the different venoms of poisonous snakes. So this was my third choice.

"For my experiment, I decided to build a wooden excavator robot that I could control by using my own hydraulics system. I used syringes filled with water connected by rubber tubes. The arm has a claw at the end, and when I push in this syringe, the water flows through the tubing into the other syringe, forcing the arm to move and the claw to close. See?" I pushed in several syringes that I'd taped to a flat board. The wooden arm moved and the claw closed around an empty water bottle.

"Wow!" Tully and Lyra said at the same time. "That is awesome!"

My classmates Abby, Xavier, Carys, and Megan came over to look at my project, too. "I bet this one wins," Javier said.

I blushed. I hoped Dad liked it as much as my friends did. "Thank you. May the best project win," I said to Carys.

Even though she smiled at me, her eyes didn't seem too happy.

Miss Flores clapped her hands three times. "Okay, class! Let's head back to Room 113. We'll come back after lunch to move our projects to the gym for tonight! I am so excited!"

I was excited, too. So excited I wanted to jump around like I was on a trampoline. And usually I am the calm one! It was going to be really hard to be patient for the next nine hours and forty-three minutes!

Chapter 2

Science Fair Fiasco

School almost always went too fast for me. I wanted to learn everything I could. Scientists need to know so much stuff it might fill up their entire brains. And maybe stuff might even fall out if they didn't stretch their brains with learning and memorizing things. Mom and Dad both said I need to start growing and stretching my brain now, and I agreed with them.

So I never let Lyra's loud whispers or Rocket throwing one of his MegaAsteroids at my head interrupt my thoughts. But I had to admit that today was a hard day to concentrate on learning stuff, even though Miss Flores is a super teacher. In math, we worked on memorizing our times tables up to twelve. In social studies, Miss Flores wanted us to learn all fifty states and their capitals for a big test before Thanksgiving. She used a program on the white board to quiz us. I got every single one correct.

For recess, we grabbed our jackets and ran outside to the playground. Most of the leaves had turned brown and fallen off the trees. Piles of them crunched under our shoes. Rocket brought out some balls and we decided to play a game of dodgeball on the basketball court.

We were dividing up teams in our regular way when Javier, Megan, and Xavier came up. "We'd like to play, too," Megan said. "Unless you think you're too good for us at dodgeball, too."

Caleb bounced the orange ball. "What does that mean?"

"I'm talking to Alex," Megan said with a smirk on her face. "He thinks he's better than us 'cause he made that really tricky science project to show off."

I shook my head. "It wasn't to show off. I love science. I did it because I wanted to."

Xavier rolled his eyes. "Everybody knows Miss Flores likes you best because you always answer all the questions right. She'll pick you to win the Science Fair because you're the teacher's pet."

"Yeah!" Megan said, her hands on her hips. "Someone should put the teacher's pet in a cage."

Caleb normally loved word jokes like that. But he didn't smile this time. "Being mean is not okay. Alex works hard to be smart. If you guys are going to act like bullies, then you shouldn't play with us right now."

Xavier and Megan glared at us. "Fine. Suit yourself," Megan said in a huffy voice. They turned and stomped away.

Rocket clapped Caleb on the back. "That was awesome!"

Caleb shrugged and grinned at me. "You've gotta stick your neck out on a limb sometimes."

"Well, thank you," I said. I pushed my glasses back up the bridge of my nose. My fingers were kind of shaky. I tried not to think about my classmates being mad at me.

We went ahead and played a great game of dodgeball. Rocket got me out three times, but I'm used to that. Dad always said my skills were in my brain.

Miss Flores blew her whistle then, and we headed back inside to put our sweatshirts and jackets in our lockers and use the drinking fountain. Caleb grunted as he tried to shut his locker, but the sleeve of his blue sweatshirt and a whole bunch of papers stuck out. Also, half of an empty juice box.

"Are you ever going to clean that thing?" Lyra asked, rolling her eyes.

"There might be interesting science experiments to conduct in there," I said, helping Caleb push on the door. "It smells funny."

"Funny as in disgusting!" Lyra leaned against Caleb's back and pushed. The locker clicked shut.

Caleb stared at his locker with a scrunched-up face. He pushed his brown hair out of his eyes and huffed, which just sent the hair right back where it was. "Um, guys? I totally left my English book in there."

Lyra and I groaned. When Caleb opened his locker again, an apple core tumbled out and rolled against Lyra's shoe. His locker held the usual school stuff like markers and notebooks, but it was also crammed with two sweaters, three skateboard wheels, a few empty soda cans, a yo-yo, and several icky socks.

"There should be a law against this!" Lyra said.

"There it is." Caleb said. He yanked out his English book. Only it had something stuck to it: a black, stinky, slimy banana peel.

"Gross!" Tully and Lyra squealed at the same time.

Caleb wiped off his math book with his shirt sleeve. He dangled the banana peel at Lyra with a mischievous grin. "What? You don't want this?"

I was trying to decide if I could use the banana peel to study the mold growth of different rotting fruits, but Lyra grabbed my arm. "Let's go before he does anything more disgusting!"

We dashed into the classroom and found our seats just as Miss Flores started language arts class. "Remember how we've been talking about the plural forms of different nouns," Miss Flores said as she wrote some words on the white board. "The plural of fox is foxes. The plural of ox is oxen. Let's review some examples. What is the plural of man, Rocket?"

"Men," Rocket answered.

"Good. And what is the plural of child?"

"Twins!" Rocket said.

Miss Flores chuckled. "Way to think outside of the box, Rocket. But I was thinking of a slightly different answer."

The rest of class went pretty quick, although it was always hard to understand why the plural of fish was still just fish, and the plural of deer was still deer. Science was so much easier to figure out.

During lunch, I could hardly eat my peanut butter and jelly sandwich. My stomach and my brain could only concentrate on the Science Fair.

Finally it was time to move our projects into the gym. We walked into the science lab.

"Brr!" Tully said, rubbing her arms. "It's cold in here!"

Suddenly Lyra yelled, "Oh no!"

Everybody pushed into the room to see what was going on. In the right side corner of the room, someone's science project had been knocked to the floor. My stomach did a painful flip flop. It was my project!

Smashed plastic and pieces of wood were scattered everywhere. My presentation poster was on the floor and bent sideways. Tully's baking soda had spilled, and white powder dusted the table and the floor. The hydraulic excavator was broken into several pieces. My science report papers fluttered in the breeze coming from the open window.

Nobody said anything for a long time. Now my science grade would be ruined. Dad wouldn't get to see how hard I'd worked to build something great. I blinked a whole bunch to hold back the beaker full of tears that wanted to spill out.

"Oh dear, oh dear," Miss Flores said, rubbing her hands together. "How in the world did this happen?"

Chapter 3

Gumshoe Gang Takes the Case

"The wind must have blown it over," Megan said, pointing at the open window.

Miss Flores walked carefully to the window and pushed it shut. Her heel crunched one of the plastic syringes. "I don't remember opening a window," she said with a frown. "Does anyone remember if it was open this morning?"

I closed my eyes, thinking back to this morning when Mom and I had set up my project. "I didn't feel any wind."

"It's cold today," Tully pointed out. "We all wore our jackets outside for recess. And it's really cold in this room, but it wasn't this morning. So the window wasn't open this morning."

Miss Flores nodded. "Very good point, Tully."

"Why would someone open a window to make the room cold?" Caleb asked.

"Maybe they wanted the wind to knock over Alex's project," Lyra said.

"Or someone destroyed the project themselves. Then they opened the window to make us think it was the wind," Tully said, narrowing her eyes.

I stared sadly at my ruined hard work. "I don't think the wooden excavator would have broken into a bunch of pieces like this just from falling off the table. Everything is smashed, not just a few things."

Miss Flores rubbed her head with her fingers. "Tully and Alex, I think you two may be right, unfortunately."

"Then this is a case for the Gumshoe Gang!" Rocket said.

"Yes," Miss Flores said. "Cheating and mean behavior will not be tolerated at the Science Fair or anywhere else. But you don't have much time to solve this mystery. Do you kids think you can figure this out before tonight?"

"Yes, we can!" The five of us said together. Caleb didn't even jinx us.

Miss Flores nodded. "Good to hear. Then I will give you a hall pass. I will move your science projects to the gym so you can get right to work. Good luck."

"So they get to miss the rest of science class?" Xavier whined. "That's not fair!"

"Solving mysteries is a form of science," Miss Flores said. "Now class, let's get to work on carefully moving all of these great projects!"

The Gumshoe Gang stood in a semi-circle around the ruined experiment, which was now officially the scene of a crime. Tully pulled her pink magnifying glass out of her back pocket and handed it to me. Then she pulled out her detective notebook. It was almost weird how she always had that thing whenever we needed it.

Tully was in charge of writing down all the notes for our cases, which was usually stuff like suspects, clues, motives, and alibis. The notebook had yellow polka-dots with REAL DETECTIVE CLUES: PRIVATE: NO PEEKING scrawled in purple marker across the front and THAT MEANS YOU! printed at the bottom.

"Okay, what clues do we see here?" Tully asked, her unicorn pencil poised over the notebook.

She examined the scene with the magnifying

glass, looking for anything out of place or unusual. "Look, there are footprints in the white powder on the floor!"

"These two must be from Miss Flores," Lyra said, pointing to a spot close to the window. We could see the outline of a heel and the front part of her shoe print from her high heels.

"But these are different," Rocket said. There were four prints from a smaller sneaker. The prints were so clear in the powder that I could even see the tread marks.

"And here's a third print!" Caleb said excitedly. "Look at these huge footprints! They look like they're made by some big bad ugly—"

"Those are your footprints!" I said.

"Oh. Oops." Caleb stepped back, lifted up his own shoe, and sheepishly brushed off the powder.

"We need to be careful we don't contaminate the evidence ourselves," Tully said, frowning at Caleb.

"I wish there was a way we could capture these other shoe prints," Lyra said. "If anyone bumps or steps into the powder, the evidence will be destroyed."

"Good idea, Lyra," Tully said. "Of the three different size prints, one type is Caleb's and one type belongs to Miss Flores. The third print type will probably belong to the culprit. This is a very important clue."

I closed my eyes and thought really hard. "We could get a measuring stick and measure the size of the prints. And Tully, you could draw the shoe print in your notebook, including as much detail as you can. You can see the wavy shape of the treads in the powder. Then we could compare the size and pattern with the shoes of any suspects."

"Oh! Like Cinderella!" Lyra clapped her hands.

Tully had just finished measuring and drawing the shoe print when the bell rang. "Okay, quick," Tully said. "Do we see anything else?"

I zoomed in close to the robot with the magnifying glass, being careful not to step into the white powder. "There's a green thread snagged on a shard of the broken wooden arm," I said. "I haven't worn anything green since I built the excavator, so I'm sure it's not mine."

Tully got a plastic baggie from one of the cabinets in the lab. I pinched the thread between my fingers and placed it in the plastic bag.

Caleb patted my shoulder. "We've got some good clues. We'll solve this case in record-breaking time. Button your seat belts!"

A Scientific Mystery

We met again during afternoon recess to discuss the case. We sat in a circle in our favorite spot in the shade beneath the slide. The wind shook the trees and whistled around the playground. The girls' hair whipped into their faces, but my hair was shaved super short, so I didn't have to worry about that.

Tully had her notebook opened in her lap. "Okay. Before we start examining shoes, we need to narrow down the suspects list."

"Do we even have a suspects' list?" Rocket asked.

"Not yet. We're making one right now. Who would have a reason to ruin Alex's Science Fair project?"

"Carys Johnson wants to win super badly because her dad will give her extra money," Lyra said.

"And Megan and Xavier we really mean at first recess," Caleb said. "Megan was jealous because she think's Alex is Miss Flores's favorite."

"So maybe one of them messed up my project for revenge," I said. I didn't like thinking about my classmates being jealous or angry at me.

Tully wrote everything down in the notebook. "Anybody else?"

"Xavier seemed worried that he would get in trouble if he didn't do really well on his project," Lyra said. "Maybe he thought ruining yours would make his look better."

"Has anyone thought of aliens yet?" Rocket asked. "Maybe they came flying through the window with their super-galactic powers. They wanted to steal the excavator arm that Alex made for their own evil purposes, only they broke it on accident."

Tully glared at Rocket. "I am not even writing that down."

We all looked at each other. We couldn't think of anybody else.

"What about one of the older kids? Or younger?" Caleb asked. "I always think those kindergarteners are up to no good."

Lyra rolled her eyes up toward the sky. "Just because you think your little sister is out to ruin your life does not mean all the other little kids are too."

Caleb shrugged. "If the shoe fits."

"Ha, ha," I said. "Speaking of shoes, I think we can tell from the length of the shoe print how big or small the suspect will be. Here, measure my shoe against the drawing." I took off my shoe and held it up to the measurement. "This print is about eight inches long. I wear a size one, and my shoe is about the same size as the suspect's."

"Eureka!" Rocket yelled. "You're the guilty party! You ruined your own project!"

"Calm down, Rocket," I said. "See, my treads are square, not wavy like the print. Besides, most third graders probably have the same shoe size."

"Measure my foot!" Caleb said. He took off his shoe and the most awful stinky sock stench filled our noses.

"Agh!" Lyra yelled, plugging her nose.

Rocket pretended to faint. "I can't breathe!"

Caleb ignored them and held up his shoe. "I'm

a size two, and my shoe is biggest."

"You have the biggest stink, too!" Tully said. "Please put that shoe back on!"

Caleb obeyed. When we'd all recovered, we looked back over our list. "So the suspect must be a third grader," Tully said. "Any other questions we should be asking?"

"Yes," Rocket said. "Why do we have armpits, and more importantly, why are they smelly?"

"No, I mean questions about the case."

"Oh. Then, nope. I've got nothing."

I squeezed my eyes shut so I could think of all the possibilities, like a scientist and a detective. "We have several suspects with motive. But what about opportunity? They went back to the science lab sometime between first thing this morning and this afternoon after lunch."

"Yes!" Tully said. She climbed to her feet and brushed off her yellow sparkly jeans. "Let's ask Miss Flores who used hall passes."

We dashed up to Miss Flores. She was holding her long dark hair back with both hands to keep it from flying all over her face in the wind. "How can I help the Gumshoe Gang?"

We told her our clues so far and asked about hall passes. She closed her eyes and scrunched up her face to show she was thinking, just like I did. "I gave a hall pass to Xavier to use the restroom during mathematics. Megan and Abby both used the drinking fountain during first recess. Aidan asked to retrieve his English book from his locker during Language Arts, and Carys went to Mr. Sleuth's office on the way down to the cafeteria because she'd forgotten her lunch box. And then, of course, I gave a hall pass to the Gumshoe Gang during science lab." She opened her eyes and smiled. Miss Flores had a really excellent memory.

Tully wrote down all the facts as speedily as she could. "This is just the information we needed!"

"Do you need a little more time? I can extend recess by ten minutes."

"Thank you so much!" Lyra and Tully said together. We huddled next to the brick wall to get out of the wind.

Tully closed her notebook. "It's time to interview our suspects!"

Chapter 5

The Plot Thickens

My stomach felt all sick and queasy, like I'd swallowed a test tube of green slime. I didn't like imagining anybody ruining my science project on purpose. I almost didn't want to know. Almost. But a good scientific detective would be able to put his feelings aside to get the job done. And I could too!

We found Carys on the swings. She skidded to a stop when we came up to her. "What's up?"

"Why did the robber take a bath before he stole from the bank?" Caleb asked.

"I don't know."

"Because he wanted to make a clean getaway!"

"Oh. That's pretty funny," Carys said. She smiled, but she looked confused too. "Why are you telling me a joke?"

Caleb narrowed his eyes at her. "Are you trying

36

to make a clean getaway, too?"

"What?"

"Never mind him," I said. "He's just being silly."

"We could use your help," Tully said. "We are trying to eliminate suspects in the case of Alex's wrecked science project."

"We know how badly you want to win!" Lyra blurted.

"Well, yeah. I could use that money to buy a really awesome easel for my paintings. But I didn't want to win badly enough to cheat, if that's what you mean."

"That sounds good," Caleb said. "But can you help us prove it?"

Rocket nudged me with his elbow. He pointed to the knit sweater Carys was wearing, which was brown with blue and green polka dots on it. "We found a green thread at the scene of the crime," I said.

Carys looked down at her shirt. "Lots of kids are wearing green today."

She had a point there.

"How about your shoes. What size are you?"

"I wear a size one. Why?"

"Aha!" Rocket cried. "You are the Science Fair bandit! Confess to everything, you scallywag!"

Tully grabbed Rocket's arm. "Rocket, not everyone who wears a size one shoe is guilty, remember?"

"Oh, yeah. Oops." Rocket looked down at the ground and shuffled his feet. "Sorry."

"But can we still see the bottom of your shoes, please?" Lyra asked.

Carys shrugged. Still sitting on the swings, she flopped her leg over her knee and tilted up the sole of her shoe. The tread of her canvas sneakers was shaped like dozens of squares with smaller circles inside them. Tully held the shoe print drawing next to Carys' shoe. No match.

"Thanks for your help," I said.

Rocket narrowed his eyes at her. "Don't even think about leaving town!"

"Ignore him," Tully said.

"Good luck!" Carys called after us as we went in search of Megan. Megan and her best friend, Emily, were sitting and whispering to each other under the big maple tree by the basketball courts.

Megan scowled at me as we walked up. "What do you want, Teacher's Pet?"

"Megan Moore. It is not okay to be a big meanie," Tully said. "You need to stop right now."

Megan crossed her arms over her chest. "Make me."

"We'll have to tell Miss Flores," Caleb said.

"You are impeding an important investigation!" Rocket said loudly. I was pretty sure he had no idea what that meant.

Megan's face got all pale, which happens when the blood drains away from the blood vessels in a person's face when they are scared. That is a scientific fact. "This is very serious crime business," I warned her.

Megan huffed a big sigh. "Okay, fine. I'll talk to you." She whispered something to Emily, who got up quickly and walked back toward the playground.

Caleb elbowed me and whispered, "That sure took the steam out of her sails!"

"You used the drinking fountain during first recess, correct?" Tully said, looking down at her notebook.

"Yes. So what?"

"Did you go anywhere else? Like to the science lab?"

"Nope. Are we done now?"

Rocket narrowed his eyes at her. "Do you speak telepathically with aliens? That means you can hear them in your head."

"What? No!"

"Next question," Tully said, glaring at Rocket. "Are you wearing anything green today?"

"Nope."

"Are you sure?"

"Yes. Why?"

"Well, your sweater is zipped all the way up, so we can't see the shirt underneath."

"Ugh! Okay, fine." Megan tugged open her sweater. Underneath, her collared shirt was green. "Whoops. I totally forgot about that. Is that a problem?"

Tully sucked in her cheeks. "Maybe. Can we also see the underside of your shoe?"

"What for?"

"It's procedure," Caleb said.

Megan rolled her eyes. "Here." She took off one of her shoes and handed it to me. I held it next to Tully's drawing. The size was the same. The tread was wavy lines, just like the drawing.

"Eureka! This one's guilty for real!" Rocket jumped up and down in excitement.

"Hold your donkeys!" Caleb said, holding up his hand. "Let Megan confess."

Megan climbed to her feet. "I'm not confessing anything! And that is not my shoe in your stupid drawing!"

"It matches perfectly! And you're wearing a green shirt. We found a green thread at the scene of the crime," I said.

Megan started shaking her head back and forth really fast. "I did not smash your stupid robotic arm thingy. Why would I do that?"

"Because you are mad and jealous of Alex," Lyra said. She pointed her finger at Megan. "You think Miss Flores likes him best, so this was a way to get revenge."

Miss Flores blew her whistle. It was time to go back inside, but Megan didn't move. "I didn't do it. And I'm not lying."

Caleb said, "If you won't tell the truth, then we'll have to tell the principal."

"Fine!" Megan snapped. She turned and stomped away. I thought I saw her wiping at her eyes.

"Now what?" Rocket asked.

I shrugged. "Now we tell Mrs. Holmes."

Missing Puzzle Pieces

Miss Flores gave us permission to visit Mrs. Holmes in her office. Mrs. Holmes was a really great principal. She was always nice unless you were in trouble. Then she turned the Holmes Eye on you, which was a stare so awful it made you feel like you might shrivel up just like a puddle evaporating in the hot sun.

Luckily for me, I never had the Holmes Eye directed at me. And luckily for the Gumshoe Gang, both Mr. Sleuth and Mrs. Holmes were meeting-free, so they could sit in the principal's office and listen to us. We told them the whole story so far, including how all the evidence pointed to Megan's guilt, but she insisted she didn't do it.

"Hmm," Mr. Sleuth said a bunch of times, stroking his chin with his fingers. Mr. Sleuth was

so tall he had to duck through doorways, which was why he sat down as much as possible.

"I'd say Megan is most definitely guilty," Mr. Sleuth said.

"Me too!" said Rocket.

"I mean, she had the motive and opportunity," Tully said. "And all the evidence points to her."

Mrs. Holmes leaned back in her leather principal's chair. "I agree with you, Tully," she said. She looked at me. "There's a 'but' though, isn't there?"

"She says she didn't do it," I said.

"And how do you feel about that?" Mrs. Holmes asked.

My stomach was still all icky, that's how I felt. "Something doesn't feel right yet," I said. "But I don't know what or why."

Mrs. Holmes nodded. "That's your good detective instinct at work, Alex. Sometimes there's another piece to the puzzle, but we just can't see it yet."

Tully threw up her hands. "But if we can't see it, then how do we know it's there? And what are we supposed to do now?"

"Those are tricky questions," Mr. Sleuth said.

Mrs. Holmes smiled. "And there are no easy answers. But I have faith in all of you. Let me ask you this. Have you talked to all of your suspects yet?"

We looked at each other. "Not yet," I said.

"Well, why don't you start there?"

"That's a great idea," Mr. Sleuth said.

We agreed. We thanked Mrs. Holmes and headed back toward Room 113. The other kids were just getting ready to go to library time with Mr. Hornswoggle. It was the last class before the end of the school day, and our last chance to solve the case before the Science Fair.

If the Shoe Fits

I asked Miss Flores if we could interview our last suspect. Because she had a break during library time, she agreed to let us talk to Xavier in the classroom while she graded papers.

We sat next to Xavier while he squirmed in his seat. "I don't know why you want to talk to me. I don't know anything."

"We just have a few questions," Tully said nicely. "Can you tell us if you used a hall pass for anything this morning?"

I noticed right away that Xavier wore a blue, white, and green striped long sleeved shirt. He tugged the sleeves over his fingers. "Just the restroom."

"And you didn't go anywhere else?" I asked.

"No. Can I go now?"

"Not yet. Can you tell us what shoe size you wear?"

"One, I think. Why?"

"Can we see them?"

Xavier scrunched up his face in a scowl, but he pulled off one of his tennis shoes and handed it to me. We compared the tread marks with the drawing. Xavier's shoes had the same wavy tread as the drawing of the suspect's shoe. Both Xavier's shoe and Megan's shoe prints looked exactly the same!

Lyra gasped. "Holy Moly!"

"Does that mean Xavier and Megan are both guilty?" Rocket asked with eyes big as golf balls.

"Not necessarily," I said. "Xavier, your shoes match the shoe prints we found at the scene of the crime. We also found a green thread, and you are wearing a green shirt."

Xavier gulped. "So?"

"You said this morning you would be in big trouble if you didn't get an A in Science," I said gently.

"You still can't prove anything!" Xavier stared down at his desk. He pulled on his sleeve again. That's when I saw the small tear in the green fabric.

"Actually, we can. I have the green thread that we found at the scene. We can pull a thread from that tear in your shirt and compare them. I think they will match. I think you know they will. The matching shoe print and the matching thread from your shirt prove that you did it."

For a long moment Xavier didn't say anything. Finally he looked up at me. "I didn't plan to," he said in a wobbly voice. "I decided to just go check on the projects and see which ones were better than mine. Alex's was the best. He is always the best in science. I try really, really hard, and I'm just no good. My dad gets mad at my bad grades. He said he was going to ground me this time."

"That sounds upsetting," Tully said.

"I felt really rotten. So I just kind of bumped Alex's stuff. The poster fell down and knocked Tully's baking soda off the table. Then I just kinda pushed the excavator a little bit. I opened the window so everybody would think the wind did it. But I guess you guys are too smart for that."

"We let the evidence show us what really happened," I said. My stomach was all twisted up. I felt a little mad and a little sad, but also a lot happy about solving the mystery.

"And now I'm in even bigger trouble than before," Xavier said glumly.

"That's why I always say you shouldn't do the crime if you can't get out of the kitchen," Caleb said.

Xavier started to cry. "I know. I shouldn't have done it. It wasn't fair to ruin your project because I was worried about my grade. I'm sorry, Alex."

I sighed. "Apology accepted, Xavier."

"We need to take you to Mrs. Holmes' office," Tully said.

Xavier nodded and wiped his face with his sleeve. "Okay."

Just then, Miss Flores stood up from her desk. She asked me to stay in the classroom, while the rest of the Gumshoe Gang left with Xavier. "Great job!" she said, patting my shoulder. Then she looked at me closer. "Is something wrong, Alex?"

Science Saves the Day!

My stomach felt like a bowl of jiggly jelly. I had to sniff a bunch of times before I could talk. Then all of a sudden I couldn't stop talking. "I don't have a project for the Science Fair anymore. I worked really hard and now it's ruined. Am I going to fail science now? And I don't want to disappoint Mom and Dad. Especially Dad. I miss him so much, and he's coming tonight. I want him to be proud of me, but it's too late for that now."

Miss Flores hugged me. "Oh, Alex, I don't think it's possible for you to get a bad grade in science. I did see your project, so you will get credit. Don't worry. Now, I think you can still have something for tonight. You spent all day today using science. In fact, you used the scientific method to solve the mystery."

"I did?"

"Yes. You observed the crime scene and asked yourself why and how your project was ruined. You deducted that the wind from the open window was not strong enough to knock your project off the table. You hypothesized that the person who stepped in the spilled powder was also the culprit. You tested your hypothesis by comparing the crime scene print with the shoes of your suspects. You also concluded that the green thread matched Xavier's shirt," Ms. Flores said.

"In real life," she continued, "detectives use forensic science to solve real crimes. I think you've done enough work for another project, don't you?"

"What do you mean?" I asked.

"Well, you are staying after school for extended day, right? I have an extra poster board. What if you write about your crime-solving process and include some of your notes and drawings? Could you get that done before tonight?"

I think I leaped five feet up in the air. "Yes! I definitely, absolutely can do that!"

Miss Flores smiled. "Great. Then I will see you tonight!"

******

The night of the Science Fair, my stomach was full of fizzy bubbles of excitement. Mom brought Dad straight from the airport. I ran to him as soon as I saw him walk through the front doors. He grabbed me up in a giant bear hug, and I wasn't even embarrassed at all. I told them everything that happened, and then I showed them my project on forensic science. Forensic is a weird word, but it seemed to really impress all the grown-ups.

Even though I didn't have an actual experiment for the competition, the judges put a big blue Honorable Mention ribbon on my poster. After the Science Fair ended, Dad took me and Mom out for ice cream. And even though today didn't happen at all like I thought it would, it still ended up being one of the best days ever.

I can't wait for the Gumshoe Gang's next mystery to solve. Maybe when I grow up, I will be a scientist and a detective at the same time. I will use forensic science to solve crimes. Now that really would be the best thing ever!

A Peek Inside Tully's Notebook

8 inches

Evidence List:
shoe print, green fiber, students who used hall passes.

Possible Motives:
Megan: jealousy Carys: desperate to win
Xavier: afraid of getting a bad grade, jealous

Megan=Guilty?????

Missing puzzle piece

Q & A with Carys

Alex: So how did your robot, Picasso, do in the Science Fair competition?
Carys: I came in first place. Thanks for asking.

Alex: Did you buy that easel?
Carys: Yes, I did, and I love it! The easel holds up my canvas so I can paint.

Alex: I'm sorry we suspected you of ruining my project.
Carys: It's okay. Some of the evidence pointed to me. You knew I really wanted to win. I used a hall pass so I had the opportunity to commit the crime. And I had green on my sweater. That makes me like a red heron or something, right?

Alex: A red herring. That's a type of fish. But it also means a clue or a suspect that is misleading or distracting. Someone who appears guilty but isn't.
Carys: That's me!

Discussion Questions

1. How did the Gumshoe Gang know it wasn't the wind that knocked over Alex's Science Fair project?
2. At first, Alex and the Gumshoe Gang suspected Carys Johnson. What evidence did they use to prove it wasn't her?
3. How was Megan unkind to Alex? How did Caleb stand up for him?
4. Why did Xavier ruin Alex's project? Is it ever okay to break someone else's things?
5. Why do you think Alex chose to forgive Xavier?

Vocabulary

Can you use each of these words in a sentence? Write each sentence on an index card. Then shuffle them up and read them out loud to make a silly, mixed-up story.

confess: to admit you have done something wrong

contaminate: to make dirty or unfit for use

examine: a careful check or inspection

excavate: to dig in the earth

forensic: using science to solve crimes

glum: gloomy and miserable

hydraulic: power created by liquid forced under pressure through pipes

investigation: to find out as much as you can about something

procedure: a way of doing something especially by a series of steps

tread: the ridges on the sole of a shoe that prevent slipping

Writing Prompt

Imagine that something you cared about was mysteriously destroyed. It could be a toy or a school project. Plant some clues at the scene of the crime. How will you use the clues to solve the case?

Websites to Visit

http://idahoptv.org/dialogue4kids/season12/
    csi/facts.cfm

http://www.sciencebuddies.org/science-fair-
    projects/project_ideas.shtml

http://pbskids.org/dragonflytv/show/
    forensics.html

About the Author

Kyla Steinkraus loves mysteries and third graders (she happens to have one at home), so writing books for this series was a perfect fit. She and her two awesome kids love to

snuggle up and read good books together. Kyla also loves playing games, laughing at funny jokes, and eating anything with chocolate in it.

About the Illustrator

I have always loved drawing from a very young age. While I was at school, most of my time was spent drawing comics and copying my favorite characters. With a portfolio under my arm, I started drawing comics

for newspapers and fanzines. After I finished my studies I decided to try to make a living as a freelance illustrator... and here I am!